Not Quite a Mermaid
MERMAID WISH

Linda Chapman lives in Leicestershire with her family and two Bernese mountain dogs. When she is not writing she spends her time looking after her two young daughters, horse riding and teaching drama.

Books by Linda Chapman

MY SECRET UNICORN Series
NOT QUITE A MERMAID Series
STARDUST Series

BRIGHT LIGHTS
CENTRE STAGE

Not Quite a Mermaid
MERMAID WISH

LINDA CHAPMAN

Illustrated by Dawn Apperley

PUFFIN

PUFFIN BOOKS

Published by the Penguin Group
Penguin Books Ltd, 80 Strand, London WC2R 0RL, England
Penguin Group (USA) Inc., 375 Hudson Street, New York, New York 10014, USA
Penguin Group (Canada), 90 Eglinton Avenue East, Suite 700, Toronto, Ontario,
Canada M4P 2Y3 (a division of Pearson Penguin Canada Inc.)
Penguin Ireland, 25 St Stephen's Green, Dublin 2, Ireland
(a division of Penguin Books Ltd)
Penguin Group (Australia), 250 Camberwell Road, Camberwell, Victoria 3124, Australia (a
division of Pearson Australia Group Pty Ltd)
Penguin Books India Pvt Ltd, 11 Community Centre, Panchsheel Park,
New Delhi – 110 017, India
Penguin Group (NZ), cnr Airborne and Rosedale Roads, Albany, Auckland 1310,
New Zealand (a division of Pearson New Zealand Ltd)
Penguin Books (South Africa) (Pty) Ltd, 24 Sturdee Avenue, Rosebank,
Johannesburg 2196, South Africa

Penguin Books Ltd, Registered Offices: 80 Strand, London WC2R 0RL, England

penguin.com

First published 2006
1

Text copyright © Linda Chapman, 2006
Illustrations copyright © Dawn Apperley, 2006
All rights reserved

The moral right of the author and illustrator has been asserted

Set in Palatino by Palimpsest Book Production Limited,
Polmont, Stirlingshire
Made and printed in England by Clays Ltd, St Ives plc

British Library Cataloguing in Publication Data
A CIP catalogue record for this book is available from the British Library

ISBN 13: 978–0–141–32055–7
ISBN 10: 0–141–32055–9

lindachapman.co.uk

To Iola and Amany, no matter how near or far . . .

Contents

Contents

Chapter One

'Electra! It's almost time for school!' Maris called.

'All right, Mum!' Electra shouted from her bedroom where she was swimming in front of her mirror. She had an old brown hat on her head, which had long strips of silvery material stuck to its brim. They hung down to the floor, covering her pink seaweed bikini. Peering through the strips, Electra turned to Splash, her pet dolphin, who was watching her. 'Do you think I look like a jellyfish, Splash?' she asked hopefully.

Splash put his grey head on one

side. 'Um . . . not really,' he replied. Splash lived with Electra and Maris, who had adopted him after his parents had died. He and Electra were always having adventures together.

Electra sighed. Splash was right. She didn't look anything like a jellyfish. She just looked like someone wearing a very strange hat. 'Oh, what am I going to do, Splash?' she exclaimed, taking the hat off. 'It's the fancy dress parade tonight and my costume's nowhere near ready.'

It was the chief of the merpeople's birthday that day and to celebrate he had organized a big party with a fancy dress parade. The merchild with the best costume was going to win a statue of a jumping dolphin carved out of white coral. Electra had seen it displayed at school and she really wanted to win it so she could give it to her mum. Her mum loved dolphins.

Electra had thought really hard about what to wear for the parade and when she'd had the idea of going as a jellyfish she'd been really pleased. No one else had thought of it. All her friends were going as normal fish. However, looking at her costume now,

she was beginning to
understand why. She
just couldn't get it to
look right. The silver
strips made great
jellyfish tentacles but
the problem was how
to attach them so that
they floated around her.

She'd tried tying them to a belt but
that just made her look as if she was
wearing a long skirt. She had tried
sticking them to her shoulders but that
just made her look as if she was
wearing a shiny cloak. *I need some way*

of making them hang from above me, like a jellyfish's tentacles hang down from its head, she thought.

'Electra!' Maris called again.

'Coming!' Electra put the hat down on her bed. 'I'm going to have to finish this off later. See you after school, Splash.'

'See you!' he called as she dived through the curtain of shells that separated her bedroom from the living area of the

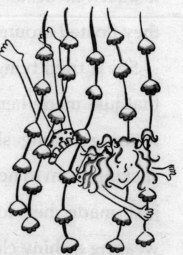

cave, her long red hair swirling around her.

'So, how's your fancy dress costume going?' Maris asked as Electra picked up her school bag.

'Not very well,' Electra admitted.

'I don't see why you don't just go as a fish,' Maris said.

'I want to be different,' Electra replied.

Maris shook her head in amused exasperation. 'Oh, Electra, don't you want to be like all the other mermaids for once?'

Electra grinned. 'That would be much

too boring!' Thinking about the dolphin statue, she hitched her school bag on to her shoulder. 'See you later, Mum!'

'Bye,' her mum called, blowing her a kiss.

Electra dived out of the cave and kicked her feet hard. Unlike the other merpeople who had long silver tails, Electra had legs. It was because she had been born a human. She had arrived at Mermaid Island on a little boat, eight years ago after a dreadful storm. She had been just a tiny baby and the merpeople had taken pity on her and rescued her. They had given her magic

sea powder so she could breathe underwater. Then Maris, who had no children of her own, had adopted her.

Sam and Sasha, the mer-twins, who lived in the cave next door to Electra, were looking out for her when she got to school. As she swam into the cave that was their classroom, they made room on the bench they were sitting on. 'Is your costume ready for tonight, Electra?' Sasha asked.

'No,' Electra replied with a sigh. 'Are yours?'

Sam nodded. 'I'm going to be a lion fish.'

'And I'm going to be an angel fish,' Sasha added proudly.

Nerissa, one of their other friends, who was sitting behind them, leant forwards. 'Are you talking about tonight?' The others nodded eagerly. 'I can't wait,' she went on. 'I'm going to be a clown fish. My mum says there's going to be a massive water slide, a basket-sponge bouncy mat you can jump on and jugglers and storytellers.'

'Yes, and the person who wins the fancy dress parade gets the dolphin statue and gets to go on everything free all night,' Sam said. 'I really want to win!'

Everyone nodded.

Just then Solon, their teacher, swam into the classroom. 'Good morning, class,' he said, clapping his hands. 'Settle down, please. Today we're going to be starting a project on shipwrecks.'

Electra sat up. Usually the projects they did at school were really boring ones, like shell identification and seaweed gardening. Shipwrecks sounded much more fun.

Nerissa raised her hand. 'There's a shipwreck out in the deep sea near here, isn't there, Solon?'

'Can we go and see it?' Electra asked eagerly. She loved going into the deep sea. Her friends didn't. They liked staying in the shallow waters where it was safe, but Electra was different from the other merchildren. She loved exploring.

Solon shook his head. 'No, we can't go. There's a trench on one side of the wreck that goes deep down into the seabed. A strong current swirls around it at this time of year.'

A shiver ran round the class. All merchildren knew about the dangers of deep-sea currents. They could sweep away even very strong swimmers. A current could pull a merperson far down into a deep-sea trench – so far that they might never get out.

'However, even though we can't visit the wreck,' Solon continued, 'I do have some things from it. They are objects that humans use but that merpeople don't.' He rummaged in a bag by his desk. 'This is a watch,' he said, holding the watch up. 'Although we use the sun to tell the time, humans use watches.' He pulled some trousers and shoes out of the bag. 'And these are things humans wear because they have legs and feet instead of tails.' Solon smiled at Electra. 'Just like Electra.'

Everyone looked round at Electra. It made her feel odd. Although she had legs she never really thought of herself as being human. She looked at the three objects. So these were things that humans used.

Solon began to pass the watch, trousers and shoes around the class. 'I'd like you all to take a good look at these objects and then choose one to draw and label for your project.'

Sam took the shoes. They were white shoes with a heel and a little bow. 'Just think, Electra. If you hadn't come to Mermaid Island, you'd live on land and wear things like these on your feet every day.'

'Yeah,' Electra replied. She wriggled her toes in the water. It was odd to

think how different her
life might have been.

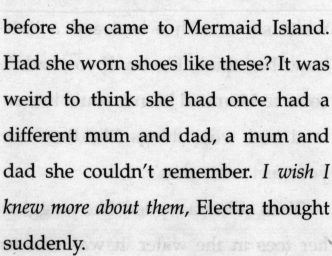

Sam passed the
shoes on to her. As
Electra took them,
she suddenly found
herself thinking about
the mum she'd had

before she came to Mermaid Island.
Had she worn shoes like these? It was
weird to think she had once had a
different mum and dad, a mum and
dad she couldn't remember. *I wish I
knew more about them*, Electra thought
suddenly.

Electra caught Solon watching her and passed the shoes on. But her mind kept returning to her parents. Her eyes widened as a thought struck her. What if they'd been on the ship that these things had come from?

Heart thudding, she stuck her hand in the air.

'Yes, Electra?' Solon said.

'How old's the shipwreck near Mermaid Island?'

'About sixty years old,' Solon replied.

'Oh.' Electra felt a rush of disappointment. So it wasn't the ship her parents had been on. That would only have been eight years old.

She put her hand down and picked up her pencil again. It would have been amazing if the wreck had been the ship her parents had been travelling on. She might have discovered some of their belongings – found out more about them. *But even if it isn't that ship*, she realized, *there might be things on it that'll show me what it's like to be human.*

She put her hand up again.

'Yes, Electra,' Solon sighed.

'Please can we go and see the wreck?' she begged him.

Solon shook his head. 'I've told you. It's too dangerous right now. Maybe in a few months.'

A few months! That was ages away.

'Now, get on with your drawing,' Solon told her.

But Electra couldn't concentrate. All she could think about was the shipwreck.

At break time she

didn't join in with the others' games.
She just stared out at the coral reef,
imagining all the interesting human
things inside the shipwreck.

'Why aren't you playing?' Sasha
asked, as the spineless sea urchin they
were playing catch with rolled to
Electra's feet.

'I don't feel like it,' Electra said.

Sasha looked at her in surprise. Electra usually loved playing games. 'Are you OK?' she asked in concern.

'I'm fine,' Electra replied distractedly. She saw Sasha's worried face. 'Really,' she insisted.

As Sasha picked up the urchin and threw it towards Hakim, Electra watched the foam breaking on the waves far out to sea. Solon had said they had to wait a few months to go to the wreck. But she definitely couldn't wait that long. She wanted to go and explore it right now.

I don't need Solon. I'm going to go on

my own, she decided. She felt a flicker of guilt at the thought of disobeying Solon. But she pushed it deep down inside her. A smile crept across her face. This was going to be a great adventure!

Chapter Two

As soon as school finished, Electra raced home. Splash was waiting for her in the garden.

'Splash!' Electra gasped. 'Do you want to have an adventure?'

'Of course!' Splash replied eagerly.

'What are we going to do?'

'Go to the shipwreck out in the deep sea!' Electra replied.

'A shipwreck!' Splash echoed. He clapped his flippers in excitement. 'When are we going?'

'Now,' Electra said.

'But what about your fancy dress

costume?' Splash asked in surprise. 'I thought you had to finish that.'

Electra hesitated. She still hadn't thought about what she could do to her costume to make it look good but going to the shipwreck seemed much more important.

'I'll have time later,' she said, waving a hand impatiently. 'The parade doesn't start till this evening.'

Maris came swimming out of the cave. 'Oh, good, you're back from school, Electra. Now, I've had an idea for your fancy dress costume. I've seen a . . .' She broke off as she saw the looks on their faces. 'You two look like you're planning something,' she said suspiciously.

'We're going on an adventure!' Splash blurted out before Electra could stop him. 'To the shipwreck in the deep sea!'

'Splash!' Electra cried in dismay. She knew her mum would say they couldn't.

She was right. Maris put her hands on her hips. 'Oh, no. It's far too dangerous!'

'We'll be very careful,' Electra said.

But Maris shook her head. 'There's

no way I'm letting you two out into the deep sea on your own.'

'But I have to go,' Electra said desperately. 'I want to . . .' She hesitated suddenly. She couldn't tell Maris that she wanted to go and find out things about her real mum and dad. After all, Maris was her mum now and Electra didn't want her to be

upset. 'Um . . . I just want to go,' she finished.

'No,' Maris said firmly.

Electra felt a wave of frustration. 'You don't understand, Mum. I *have* to go!'

'The answer's no, Electra,' Maris said.

'But I have to go!' Electra's voice rose to a shout and she stamped her foot. 'It's not fair!'

'That will do!' Maris looked cross.

'I won't have you speaking to me like that. Go to your room.'

Tears springing to her eyes, Electra swam inside.

Splash went to follow her but Electra heard Maris stop him. 'No,' Maris said. 'If Electra's going to behave rudely, she can stay on her own.'

Splash whistled in protest but Maris was firm.

Reaching her bedroom, Electra burst into tears. This was so unfair!

'Electra?' she heard Maris say from the other side of the shell curtain. Electra didn't answer.

'I'm going out,' Maris said. 'I want to get something before the shops close. But I'll be back soon. I think we need to have a talk.'

Electra didn't say anything.

She heard Maris get her things and leave the cave. Fresh tears prickled Electra's eyes. *She doesn't even care that I'm upset*, she thought. *She doesn't even care that I'm crying.*

Splash poked his head round the curtain. 'Your mum's gone out. Are you OK, Electra?'

'Yes,' Electra said in a shaky voice. 'Oh, Splash,' she said, hugging him as

he swam over. 'I want to go to the shipwreck so much.'

'Why?' he asked curiously.

'I want to see the human stuff inside.' Electra swallowed. 'My mum and dad were human and I want to know more about what they were like. If I go to the shipwreck I'll be able to find out.'

'Oh,' Splash said.

Electra stood up. 'Well, Mum's not going to stop me. I'm going to go.' She looked at him. 'Will you come with me?'

Splash flicked his tail and grinned. 'Of course I will,' he said.

Chapter Three

Mermaid Island was encircled by a coral reef that acted like a wall, keeping out all the dangerous creatures that lived in the deep sea. There was a gate in the reef but Electra knew that the adult merpeople would stop her if she tried to swim out of it. Instead she dived down until she found a hole in the coral wall. She'd got out this way once before. It was tricky because the coral was sharp. She wriggled her way through the gap, trying not to scratch herself. At last she was out in the deep sea.

As Electra swam to the surface, Splash leapt over the coral wall and plunged into the sea beside her. His dark eyes sparkled. 'Come on, let's go to the wreck!' he exclaimed.

Electra looked at the ocean stretching out around them and felt a thrill run from her head to her toes. She grabbed on to Splash's fin and he pulled her through the water. It was great fun. They zoomed downwards, going deeper and deeper, the water changing from turquoise to indigo blue around them. Splash could go so much faster than Electra on her own.

The sea grew cold and very dark. Electra felt tentacles of the deep-sea firs that grew on the bottom of the sea brushing against her toes.

'Stop!' she said quickly to Splash. Last time they had come here he had got tangled up in the tentacles. 'I'll go and find us some mermaid fire so we can see our way to the bottom.'

Electra dived down. Every so often she had to peel the clinging sea fir tentacles away as they tangled round her arms and legs. However, finally her hands reached the rock of the seabed.

'From the deep of the sea, mermaid fire come to me,' Electra murmured.

Her fingers tingled with warmth and out of the rocks flowed a stream of green fire. It formed a ball in her hands. Electra held it up like a light and looked around. Huge sea firs rose like trees out of the sand, and around them were strange rocks that had been carved by the sea into twisty shapes. Through the forest of sea firs, Electra glimpsed the hull of the sunken ship. Her heart leapt with excitement. She couldn't wait to start exploring it!

Using the ball of fire to light the way, she swam up through the dark water to where Splash was waiting.

'The wreck's over there,' Electra said, pointing downwards.

With the light from the mermaid fire it was much easier to avoid the sea firs' tentacles. Electra and Splash dived towards the wreck. Its dark wooden sides loomed over them.

'Wait!' Electra said suddenly. She grabbed Splash's fin and stopped him. 'Solon said there was a deep-sea trench somewhere near the wreck.' She looked warily around. 'I wonder where it is.'

Splash made a clicking sound in the water. Splash, like all dolphins, could find things in the water by sending a noise out into the sea and listening to the echo that came back. 'There,' he said suddenly. He nodded towards the pointed front of the ship that was jutting upwards directly in front of them. 'The water under there doesn't seem normal.'

He clicked his tongue and listened again. 'Yes,' he said confidently. 'The trench is just under the front of the boat. It's in the shadows which is why we didn't see it.'

Electra peered through the water. Now Splash was telling her where to look, she could see a wide dark crack in the shadows. The water swirled in strange patterns above it. The hole looked big enough for a mermaid to be sucked into.

As Electra watched, a long piece of purple seaweed floated by. The current grabbed the seaweed and pulled it down into the gaping trench. The seaweed didn't come back.

Electra gulped, feeling very glad that Splash was with her. It would have been easy to swim right up to the

trench without noticing until it was too late. She didn't want to be like the seaweed. 'Let's swim round and explore the boat from the other side,' she said hastily.

Keeping well away from the sea trench, they swam round the ship. The sides were damaged and rotting and the mast that would have held the main sail was broken. There were portholes running along the sides. Electra peered into one. She couldn't see anything. Inside the ship there was just a still, inky blackness. Electra shivered. There could be anything lurking in there. 'It looks a bit spooky,' she said uncertainly.

Splash swam up beside her. 'Are we going to go in?'

Electra hesitated. 'I guess it would be silly to come all this way and not explore.'

'But there might be something dangerous inside,' Splash said. 'Giant squid, moray eels, sharks . . .'

'We can't just turn round and go home,' Electra pointed out. Taking a deep breath she swam towards the porthole. 'I'm going in!' She dived bravely into the ship with her ball of fire.

Almost at once, there was a bright

blue flash and two angry yellow eyes glared at Electra through the gloom. She gasped.

It was an electric eel! Opening its wide, angry-looking mouth, the eel shot straight towards her, its body crackling with stinging electricity.

With a squeal, Electra dived out of the way. The eel whipped past her.

'Watch out, Splash!' Electra cried.

Splash leapt out of the way as the eel shot through the porthole. With an angry shake of its head it swam off through the water.

'That was close!' Electra gasped,

swimming out of the porthole to check Splash was OK.

'It only just missed me!' Splash said. 'I don't know if we should do any more exploring, Electra. There might be other dangerous things inside and . . .' He broke off and stiffened. 'Hang on. I can hear someone! Someone's coming this way, calling your name.'

'Who?' Electra asked in astonishment.

Splash clicked his tongue and concentrated hard. His

eyes widened in alarm. 'It's your mum!'

'Oh, no!' Electra gasped. 'She must have guessed this is where we'd come. If she finds us we'll be in really big trouble. Quick, Splash! We've got to hide!'

Chapter Four

Electra looked around. There was only one place they could go.

'In the ship!' she exclaimed. 'Come on, Splash!'

'But there might be more electric eels inside!' Splash whistled in alarm.

'I'd rather meet them than Mum!' Electra said, and she dived inside.

Splash followed her. It was a squeeze for him with his round dolphin tummy. 'Help!' he gasped, as he got wedged halfway through the porthole.

Electra grabbed him by the fins and pulled. He flicked his tail and swam

through the hole just as Maris came into sight.

She looked very worried. 'Electra! Splash! Are you there?'

'Ssh, Splash!' Electra hissed, her heart pounding. 'Don't say a word!'

They watched as Maris spotted the wreck and began to swim towards it. 'Electra?'

Electra swallowed. Her throat felt dry and her stomach felt as though it was curling up in knots.

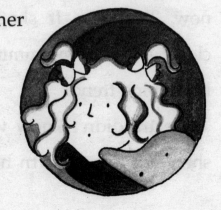

They mustn't be found. They'd be in such trouble! She watched as Maris swam closer.

'Electra!' Splash gasped. 'The sea trench! Your mum probably doesn't know it's there!'

Electra watched in horror as Maris flicked her tail and swooshed up to the front of the boat. 'Electra, if you're in that ship, come out!' Maris was near now. Too near. If she swam much closer she'd be swimming right over the gaping trench.

Electra didn't know what to do. If she went out to warn her mum then

Maris would know she was at the wreck, but if she didn't . . .

Maris swam closer. An image of the seaweed being tossed around and dragged down into the hole flashed through Electra's brain. She couldn't bear it any longer. 'Mum!' she shouted, diving out of the porthole. 'Stop!'

But it was too late. Maris had swum too far and, in an instant, the current had grabbed her. The relief that crossed Maris's face when she saw Electra quickly changed to a look of panic. She cried out in shock as she was sucked downwards.

'I'm coming!' Electra cried, plunging towards her. 'Hold on, Mum!'

'No!' Maris shouted. 'I can get free on my own!' Her tail flicked from side to side as she struggled to break from the current's grip. But the current was strong and it pulled her down towards the gaping trench.

'Mum!' Electra screamed. Not

caring about the
danger she dived
forward to help her
mum.

'Electra! Stay back!'
Maris cried. With an
enormous swish of her
tail she struggled free,
whooshing upwards just as
Electra reached her.

'You've done it, Mum. You've . . .
whoaaaa!' Electra broke off with a yell
as the current wrapped round her
legs. She tried to fight, but the current
felt like ropes pulling her down. She

kicked
hard but
she wasn't a strong
enough swimmer
to fight against the current.

'Electra!' she heard her mum shout in fear.

'Help!' Electra shrieked. She couldn't get out. She was being sucked further and further down into the cold, black depths of the sea trench!

Chapter Five

Electra's hands grasped at the water but there was nothing to hold on to. She had no way of saving herself. What was she going to do?

Suddenly her fingers brushed against a rope-like branch. Realizing that it was a tentacle of a sea fir, Electra grabbed it desperately, hoping to stop herself. But the current was still too strong. It continued to drag her downwards. The sea fir ripped through her grasp.

'No!' Electra shouted as her fingers reached the very end of the tentacle. She was going to have to let go of the sea fir!

But just then she felt the sea fir being tugged upwards. Electra gasped and held on with all her might. The sea fir moved. Someone was pulling it upwards. Hanging on desperately,

Electra felt herself being pulled
out of the depths, rising
back towards the
mouth of the hole
and freedom.

Fingers closed round
Electra's wrists. A strong silver tail
swished overhead. 'Mum!' Electra
exclaimed, looking up into Maris's
determined face at the top of the trench.

'It's OK,' Maris gasped, hanging on
to her. 'I've got you. Kick as hard as
you can!'

Electra kicked frantically. Maris's
tail flicked strongly from side to side

as, inch by inch, she pulled Electra out. First Electra's head came out of the trench, then her shoulders, then her legs and feet until then, with a final swish and a kick they fought free of the current and swooshed upwards, out of its reach.

Electra threw her arms round her mum. Her heart was pounding. 'You saved me! Oh, Mum!'

'Oh, Electra,' Maris pulled her close and hugged her tight as if she was never going to let her go. 'I thought I was going to lose you. You shouldn't have tried to help me when the current caught me. You should have left me to get out on my own.'

'I couldn't do that,' Electra exclaimed.

Maris pulled back and looked at her for a long moment. 'I know,' she said softly. She kissed Electra's hair and then her voice changed. 'Though quite what you were doing here in the first place, I'm not sure. I forbade you and Splash from exploring the shipwreck!'

Electra's eyes widened. 'Splash!' she exclaimed.

'I'm still here!' Splash whistled. He was wedged half in and half out of a porthole. 'I'm stuck,' he added unnecessarily.

Maris and Electra grinned and swam over to pull him out.

With each of them pulling on a fin, he popped out like a cork from a bottle. 'That's better!' Splash said in relief. He nuzzled Electra. 'I'm glad you're OK. And you, Maris,' he said, pushing his nose into Maris's hand. 'How did you know we were here?'

'I guessed when I couldn't find either of you at home,' Maris said. She looked at Electra. 'Why *did* you want to come here so much? Why was it so important?'

Electra looked at the sand. 'I . . .' She tried to think of some way around the question but couldn't. She swallowed, and whispered, 'I wanted to find out about my other mum and dad.' She felt better as soon as the words were out. 'I just wanted to see if I could find any other human stuff so I could see how they lived.'

Maris sighed. 'I thought it might be

something like that. You seemed so determined to come here. I decided to talk to you when I got home but when I returned you'd both gone.' She took Electra's hand. 'I know it must be hard not knowing about your real parents, Electra. I wish I could tell you about them and about what happened, but all I know is what I've always told you, that you arrived one morning in a boat after a storm. I don't know where you came from or how you got to Mermaid Island but,' she squeezed Electra's fingers, 'I do know, I've loved you ever since.'

Their eyes met and they smiled. Suddenly Electra felt much happier. She leant her head against her mum.

'I wish I could remember them,' she said quietly. 'Do you . . . do you think they loved me?'

'I'm sure they did,' Maris said. 'But that love hasn't gone away.' She turned Electra round so she was facing the sea. 'Shut your eyes. You can join in with this, Splash. I know you miss your mum and dad too.' Splash swam over and he, like Electra, shut his eyes.

'Can you feel the water all around you?' Maris asked them. Electra and Splash both nodded. 'That's what love is like,' Maris said softly. 'Even if the people you love aren't with you, their love still surrounds you. It's like the sea, it never goes away.' She paused. 'Do you understand? It's always there.'

'Yes,' Electra whispered. 'I understand.' And Splash nodded.

Maris smiled. 'Good.' Her voice

changed and became brisker. 'Now, seeing as we're here, shall we have a quick look round this shipwreck?'

Electra opened her eyes in surprise. 'Aren't you going to make us go straight home?'

'Now we're here we might as well have a look,' her mum said. 'I know how much you want to find out about the human world.'

'But what about the eels and things inside?' Splash asked.

Maris smiled. 'I'm here. You needn't worry about those.'

Electra watched as Maris gathered

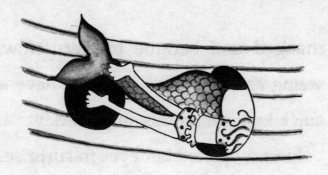

an enormous ball of mermaid fire from the seabed and then they swam in through the porthole together.

The sparkling green glow from the mermaid fire lit up the ship, showing strange objects, some that were just like things the merpeople had in their caves. There was stuff for eating – cups, plates, knives and forks – and clothes and jewellery. But there were also some other things that looked most peculiar. Electra found another watch like the one Solon had shown them but her best find was a metal pole with a curved handle and silver material rolled up around it. Electra pulled it out of a stand on the floor. There was a catch near the handle that moved. Electra pushed it all the way to the top of the pole and gasped with surprise as the material opened with a snap into a canopy above her head.

'What's that?' Splash said, staring.

'It's an umbrella,' Maris replied.

'What do humans use it for, Mum?' Electra asked.

'To keep the rain off their heads,' Maris told her. 'They don't like getting wet.'

Electra and Splash looked at each other. 'Weird!' they both said.

Electra twirled the umbrella in her hand. As the canopy twirled round an idea flashed into her mind – a brilliant, fantastic idea. A human might use an umbrella to keep the rain off but she was going to do something completely different. 'Can I take this home, Mum?'

'Yes, but why do you want it?' Maris asked.

Electra grinned. 'For my jellyfish costume!'

Splash and Maris stared at her.

'Don't you see?' Electra held the umbrella above her head. 'If I attach my silver strips to it, they'll hang down around me and I'll look *just* like a jellyfish!'

'Oh, yes!' Maris cried.

'It'll look great!' Splash exclaimed.

'Let's go back,' Electra said eagerly.

'Are you sure you've had enough of a look round?' Maris asked her.

Electra nodded. It was fun to see all the human stuff and amazing to think that she had come from that world, but she didn't feel as if she wanted to stay any longer. 'Yes,' she replied. 'I want to go home now, Mum.'

Splash turned a somersault. 'We'd better hurry!' he exclaimed. 'Or you're going to be late for the fancy dress parade!'

Chapter Six

Splash, Maris and Electra raced back to Mermaid Island. When they reached their cave, Maris swooped in and picked up a bag from the table in the living room.

'Here,' she said to Electra. 'I

bought this for you today.'

Electra looked inside. There was something silvery in there. She pulled it out. It was a beautiful bikini. 'Oh, Mum!' she gasped.

'I saw it in the shops and thought it would look much better under your jellyfish costume than your pink bikini,' Maris's eyes met Electra's. 'It was what I had gone to get when you decided to visit the wreck.'

Electra felt guilty. And she'd

thought her mum just didn't care! 'Thank you!' she said, throwing her arms round her.

Maris smiled and hugged her back. 'Hurry up and get changed now. Splash and I can stick the tentacles to the umbrella while you're getting ready.'

'OK,' Electra said eagerly. She plunged into her room with her new bikini. Her heart was pounding with excitement. What was her costume going to look like? She couldn't wait to find out!

Ten minutes later, Electra was

dressed and ready. 'Wow! Oh, wow!' she breathed as she looked in the mirror. Her new silver bikini fitted her perfectly and her mum had tied some spare bits of silver material into bows in her hair. Over her head she held the open umbrella. Her mum and Splash had stuck the silver streamers all around the edge. They fell to the floor, looking just like a jellyfish's tentacles. To finish the costume off, her mum had drawn two big jellyfish eyes on the umbrella.

'So, what do you think?' Maris asked.

Electra beamed. 'It's perfect!' she said happily. She shut the umbrella to make it easier to swim with. 'Let's go to the party!'

The party was taking place in the market square. It was dark and the square was lit by huge torches of mermaid fire. There were mermen swimming past juggling sea cucumbers, mermaids offering round trays of seaweed biscuits shaped like starfish and a band of merpeople in one corner playing music on coral pipes and sharkskin drums. On one side of the square, a huge bouncy slide had been made out of bright blue and purple sea sponges and there was a table where people could go to get their faces painted with pictures of tiny sparkly sea horses. Shoals of fish darted around, their brightly-coloured bodies glowing in the green light cast by the mermaid fire.

In the centre of the parade, the chief of the merpeople sat on a platform on a mother-of-pearl throne, watching the contestants gather for the fancy dress parade. Beside him was a table with the beautiful white statue of the dolphin.

'It's a lovely prize,' Maris said, looking admiringly at the glittering statue. She kissed Electra. 'Good luck!'

'Thanks!' Electra called, diving away to join her friends.

Sam, Sasha, Nerissa and Hakim had all made fins for their backs and were wearing fish masks.

'Hi, Electra,' Sasha said, looking relieved to see her. 'We were wondering where you were.'

Sam looked at Electra's silver bikini

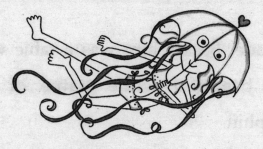

and rolled up umbrella in surprise. 'What have you come as?'

Electra opened the umbrella with a snap. 'I'm a jellyfish!' she announced.

'Wow!' her friends exclaimed as the silver strips streamed out all around Electra. They looked just like tentacles floating in the water.

'You look fantastic!' Sasha said.

'What is it?' Hakim asked, staring at the umbrella.

'An umbrella,' Electra told him.

'Humans use them when it rains because they don't like getting wet!'

Her friends looked at each other and giggled.

Just then, Solon blew the conch shell. 'The fancy dress parade will now begin!' he announced.

The musicians struck up a lively tune and all the merboys and mergirls began to parade around the square. As Electra swam round with the umbrella over her head and the silver strips floating around her, she could see people pointing and hear their gasps of surprise. Electra grinned and waved. She was having such a good time that she didn't notice the chief standing up to announce the winner until Sasha nudged her.

'Thank you all for coming to celebrate my birthday,' the chief said in his booming voice. 'I hope you're all having a wonderful time.' He lifted his trident. 'I am now going to announce the winner of the fancy dress parade. I have chosen . . .' He paused and then pointed his trident straight at Electra. 'Electra!'

Electra gasped in delight. Sasha and Nerissa squealed and hugged her.

Hands pushed her forward towards the chief's platform.

She walked up the steps and stood before him. He beamed at her. 'Well, Electra, your costume is certainly very different. I've never seen anyone dressed as a jellyfish before and I've certainly never seen anyone use a human umbrella in their costume. Congratulations.'

'It wasn't just me who made my

costume. I couldn't have done it without my mum and Splash.' Electra looked towards her mum and Splash. Splash clapped his flippers and Maris looked very pleased.

'Well done to you all.' The chief handed her the beautiful dolphin statue.

'Thank you,' Electra breathed in delight as everyone cheered.

Buzzing with happiness, Electra left the platform. People patted her on the back and clapped as she made her way to her mum.

'Well done!' Maris cried.

'You won, Electra!' Splash exclaimed.

'It's thanks to both of you. I'd never have been ready in time if you hadn't helped me,' Electra said.

'The dolphin's gorgeous,' Maris said, looking at the statue.

'It's for you, Mum,' Electra said, putting it into her mum's hands. 'It's why I wanted to win so badly,' she explained. 'I wanted you to have it.'

Maris looked speechless for a moment and then her eyes filled with tears. 'Thank you, Electra,' she whispered. 'It's beautiful.'

Electra smiled. 'I love you, Mum.'

'I love you too,' Maris said, hugging her.

Behind them the music started up again. People began to head to the centre of the square to dance.

Ronan, the twins' dad, swam over. 'Would you like to dance, Maris?'

Maris smiled. 'That would be lovely.' She dropped a kiss on Electra's head. 'See you later.' She took Ronan's hand and they swam off.

Electra put her arm round Splash and watched her mum put the statue down carefully and start to dance. 'Do you remember what Mum said, Splash? About love.'

'Being like the sea,' Splash replied.

Electra nodded. 'I liked what she said – that it doesn't go away. It surrounds you forever.'

Splash looked at her. 'Do you think it's true?'

They stood for a moment feeling the sea swirl around them.

'Yes,' Electra said softly, thinking about the parents she couldn't remember. 'I do.'

She rested her head against Splash's and they stood for moment, both lost in thought until Sam, Sasha, Nerissa and Hakim came swooshing up to them.

'Come on, you two! Come and dance!' Sasha said. She grabbed Electra's hands and pulled her towards the dancing area that was now lit by hundreds of tiny fluorescent blue jellyfish. The others followed. Reaching the dance floor they took each other's hands and spun round in a circle with Splash diving in and out of their legs.

I'm so lucky to live here, Electra

thought as she twirled around. *I've got Mum, Splash and all my friends. What more could I want?*

Nothing, she realized. And laughing in delight, she held on tight to her friends' hands, spinning round and round as the sea blurred to a sparkling blue glow around them.

Do you love magic, unicorns and fairies?

Join the sparkling

Linda Chapman

fan club today!

It's FREE!

You will receive a sparkle pack, including:

Stickers   **Badge**

Membership card   **Glittery pencil**

Plus four Linda Chapman newsletters every year,
packed full of fun, games, news and competitions.
And look out for a special card on your birthday!

How to join:

Visit lindachapman.co.uk and enter your details

Send your name, address, date of birth* and email address (if you have one) to:
**Linda Chapman Fan Club, Puffin Marketing,
80 Strand, London, WC2R 0RL**

Your details will be kept by Puffin only for the purpose of sending information regarding Linda Chapman
and other relevant Puffin books. It will not be passed on to any third parties.
You will receive your free introductory pack within 28 days

*If you are under 13, you must get permission from a parent or guardian

Notice to parent/guardian of children under 13 years old: Please add the following to their email/letter including
your name and signature: I consent to my child/ward submitting his/her personal details as above.